esented to

ranker...

KIMBERLY DERTING and SHELLI R. JOHANNES

Cece
LOVES SCIENCE

Illustrations by

VASHTI HARRISON

Greenwillow Books, an Imprint of HarperCollins Publishers

Ceco loved to ask questions.
Her mother said her first word was "Why?"
Her father said it was "How?"
But her favorite question was "What if?"

"You would make a great scientist, Cece,"
said her teacher, Ms. Curie. "Because science
is all about asking questions."

"Do fish ever get thirsty?" Cece wanted to know.

"They do," said Ms. Curie.

"Do hummingbirds really hum?"

"The sound comes from their wings," said Ms. Curie.

"What if we all jumped at the same time? Would the earth move?"

"Good question," said Ms. Curie. "I think we should investigate!"

Ms. Curie told Cece and her friends about famous
scientists from history, such as Caroline Herschel,
Thomas Edison, George Washington Carver,
and Jane Goodall.

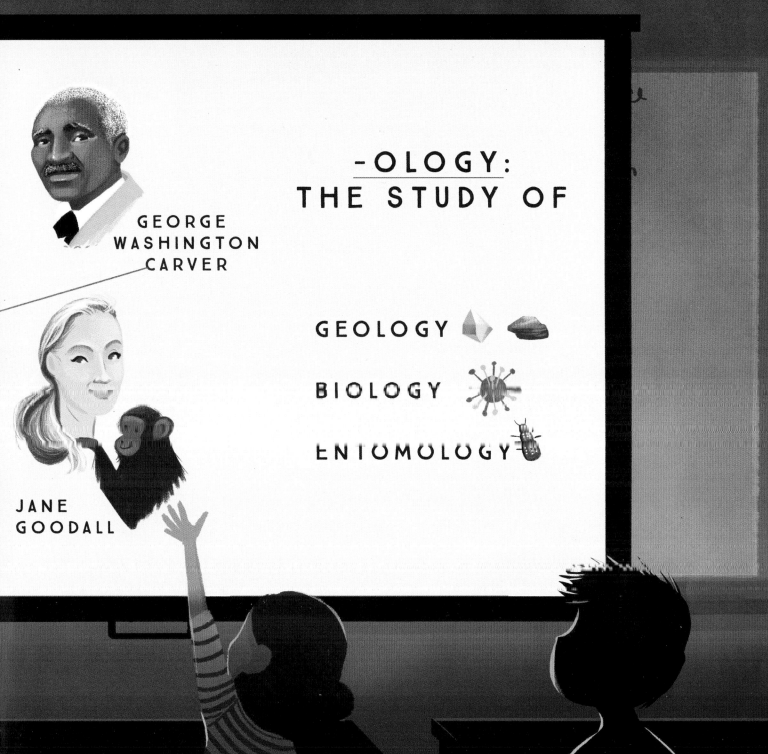

She also introduced them to many different sciences.
Geology is the study of the earth.
Biology is the study of living things.
Entomology is the study of insects.

One day, Ms. Curie told everyone to pair up.
"For our next project, I'd like you to pick a science
you are curious about, and come up with a question
to investigate," she said.
Cece and her best friend Isaac were a team. They
both loved zoology, which is the study of animals.
Now they just needed to think of an interesting
question.

First, they brainstormed
a bunch of ideas.
Science is all about possibilities.
"Is a bear ticklish?" Cece asked.
"Do we really want to find out?" said Isaac.
"Do pigs know when they are smelly?" Cece asked.
"Only a pig can answer that," Isaac said.
"Keep thinking," said Ms. Curie. "A scientist thinks
outside the box and never, ever gives up."

That night at dinner, Cece was explaining the project to her parents when her dog Einstein jumped up and started eating the food right off her plate.

"Einstein! Down!" said Cece's mother.

Cece giggled. Her plate was licked clean, except for the broccoli. "Look what Einstein did!" she said.

"I guess neither of you likes your veggies," her dad said, laughing.

This observation gave Cece a great idea.
Einstein could be their science project!
Cece called Isaac. "I've got it! Let's find out
if dogs eat vegetables."
"Cool!" said Isaac.
Cece couldn't wait to get started.

The next day, after school, Cece and Isaac headed straight to Cece's lab to work on their project.

MS. CURIE'S SCIENCE PRO...
WORKSHEET Cece + Isaac

SCIENCE: Zoology, the study of Animals.

BRAINSTORM IDEAS: Is a bear ticklish? Do pigs think they stink? Do fish sleep?

WHAT IS YOUR QUESTION?
Do dogs eat vegetables?

YOUR TEST SUBJECT: Dogs - Canis. Related to the wolf, coyote.

LIST SOME FUN FACTS ABOUT YOUR SUBJECT:
Einstein named after Albert Einstein
Weight: 40lbs
Color: gray
Eyes: brown

"What do we do first?"
asked Isaac.
"Let's observe our subject,"
Cece said.

"Observation: Doggie treats
guarantee one-hundred-percent
participation," said Cece.
"Excellent data," said Isaac.

Isaac and Cece watched
Einstein eat.

They watched Einstein drink.

They even watched Einstein sleep.

Sometimes science was all about waiting . . .
and waiting . . . and waiting . . .
for something really cool to happen.

"From our observations, we know Einstein loves
to eat kibble and doggie treats," said Cece.
"Now we need to investigate our question," said Isaac.
"Do dogs eat vegetables?"

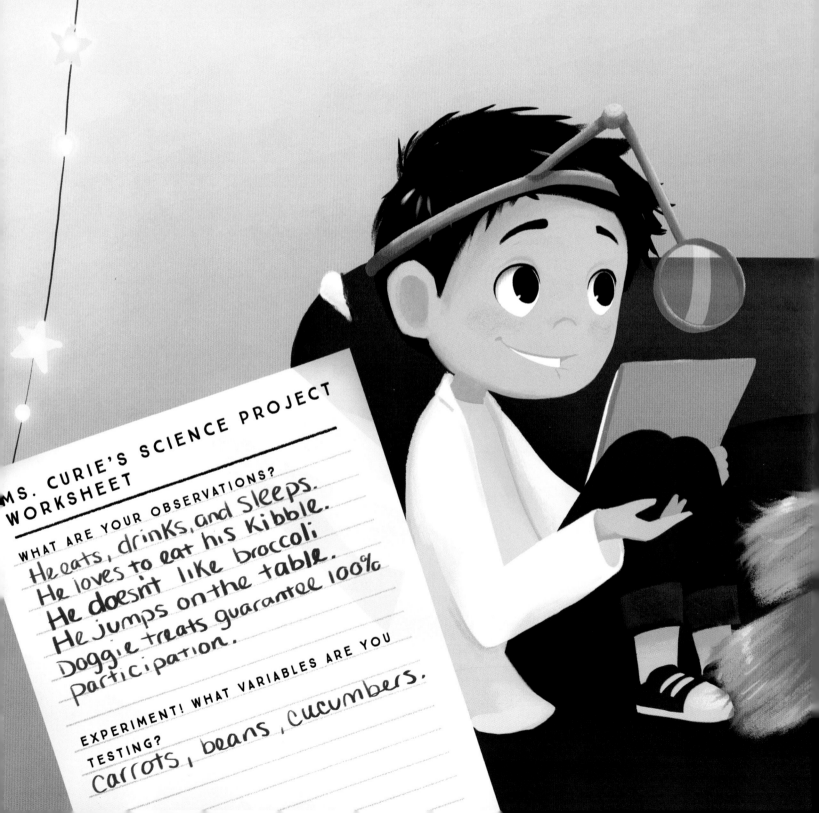

MS. CURIE'S SCIENCE PROJECT WORKSHEET

WHAT ARE YOUR OBSERVATIONS?

He eats, drinks, and sleeps.
He loves to eat his kibble.
He doesn't like broccoli.
He jumps on the table.
Doggie treats guarantee 100%
participation.

EXPERIMENT! WHAT VARIABLES ARE YOU TESTING?

carrots, beans, cucumbers.

"I already know Einstein doesn't like broccoli,"
said Cece. "I don't either."

"Let's test some different veggies," said Isaac.

"It's experiment time!" said Cece. "Finally!"

Cece and Isaac tried carrots, beans, and cucumbers. Einstein turned up his nose at each one.

"What if we disguise the vegetables with bacon and ketchup?" Isaac asked. This time, Einstein was interested. He ate the bacon and licked the ketchup off the vegetables.

"That means he likes bacon and ketchup," said Cece.

"What if we just mix up vegetables with his
  kibble?" asked Isaac.
"I bet he won't even know the difference,"
  said Cece.

Einstein ate all his kibble,
but left the vegetables
in the bottom of his bowl.
"Einstein might not eat
vegetables, but he sure
is smart!" said Cece.

Cece gave Einstein a treat and rubbed his ears.
"Good boy," she said.

She looked at Isaac and shrugged. "Now what?"

"We're supposed to interpret our data," said Isaac.

"Einstein *definitely* loves to eat!" said Cece.

"He sure doesn't like broccoli," said Isaac.

"He doesn't like *any* vegetables," added Cece.

"Not even if we cover them in bacon and ketchup,"
said Isaac.

"I guess Einstein is a picky eater," said Cece.

That night at dinner, Cece was so disappointed she
didn't even finish her dessert.

"Maybe I'm not a real scientist after all," she said.

"Our project was boring."

"I thought you asked a great question," her dad said.
Einstein put his paws on the table and sniffed Cece's
banana split.

"Einstein!" Cece giggled. "Naughty puppy!"

Her mother laughed and pulled Einstein away.

"He may not eat veggies," she said. "But he sure likes
bananas!"

That's when Cece remembered something Ms. Curie
always said—scientists think outside the box.
"What if we create a secret recipe using bananas?"
she asked.

Cece and Isaac rushed home after school and mixed together carrots, beans, cucumbers, and bananas in a blender.

"Are those still veggies?" asked Isaac.

"Yup," said Cece. "They're just in a different form."

"Gross," Isaac said, wrinkling his nose.

Cece poured the mixture into Einstein's bowl. "How about a special smoothie?" she asked, patting his head.

At first Einstein looked confused.
He circled the bowl.

He sniffed the bowl.

Then he got down on his belly and wagged his tail.

And then he slurped down the entire thing!

"Look! He loves it!" said Isaac.

In science, not all results are totally predictable.

"Einstein does eat vegetables *when* we mix them
with bananas," said Cece.

And that's when Cece made the most
extraordinary observation of all.
Science isn't just about asking questions . . .
real scientists have fun finding answers, too.

MS. CURIE'S SCIENCE PROJECT WORKSHEET

SCIENCE: Zoology, the study of animals

BRAINSTORM IDEAS: Is a bear ticklish? Do pigs think they stink? Do fish sleep?

WHAT IS YOUR QUESTION? Do dogs eat vegetables?

YOUR TEST SUBJECT: Dogs - Canis. Related to the wolf, coyote.

LIST SOME FUN FACTS ABOUT YOUR SUBJECT:
Einstein, named after Albert Einstein
Weight: 40lbs   Color: gray   Eyes: brown

WHAT ARE YOUR OBSERVATIONS?
· He eats, drinks, and sleeps
· He loves to eat his kibble
· He doesn't like broccoli
· He jumps on the table.
Doggie treats guarantee 100% Participation

EXPERIMENT! WHAT VARIABLES ARE YOU TESTING?
1ST EXPERIMENT: Carrots, beans, cucumbers, Bacon, and Ketchup
2ND EXPERIMENT: Add bananas. Mix with veggies to make a smoothie.

INTERPRET YOUR DATA:
· Eats bacon, Ketchup, and kibble.
· Ignores hidden vegetables
· Einstein is a picky eater.

RESULT: Doesn't like veggies, carrots, beans, cucumbers
Einstein does eat vegetables when we mix them with bananas!

Cece's Science Facts

- **Biology**—The study of living things. This includes plants, animals, and fungi. It also includes bacteria and viruses, which can make us sick . . . gross!

- **Brainstorm**—To come up with tons of awesome ideas.

- **Caroline Herschel**—An astronomer who discovered eight comets. Six of them were even named after her!

- **Data**—A collection of facts for an experiment.

- **Einstein**—My dog and test subject. He was named after Albert Einstein, a famous scientist who had wild hair and tons of theories in math and physics.

- **Entomology**—The branch of zoology that studies insects.

- **Experiment**—A scientific test to investigate questions and find answers.

- **Geology**—The study of the earth and what it's made of.

- **George Washington Carver**—He studied botany (the study of plants) and was known as the "Plant Doctor."

- **Interpret**—To explain the meaning of information that has been collected.

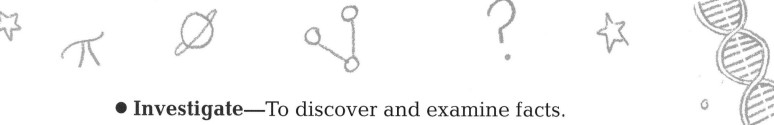

- **Investigate**—To discover and examine facts.

- **Jane Goodall**—She is an expert on chimpanzees. She even lived with them in Tanzania (that's in Africa)!

- **Lab** (another word for laboratory)—The special place where real scientists make really cool stuff happen. I have my very own lab.

- **Ms. Curie**—My teacher, who amazingly has the same name as the famous scientist, Marie Curie, the first woman to win the Nobel Prize and the only woman to win it twice—in physics AND in chemistry!

- **Observation**—Information you gather by watching something or someone.

- **Results**—The outcome, which sometimes can be totally unexpected.

- **Scientist**—A person who studies science. (I'm going to be a very famous one someday!)

- **Test subject**—A person, place, or thing being tested. (Dogs included!)

- **Thomas Edison**—An inventor famous for inventing the phonograph (that's a record player), the motion-picture camera (for making movies), and the lightbulb.

- **Variable**—A part of an experiment that can be changed in order to test out a hypothesis.

- **Zoology**—The study of animals and animal life.

To all the inspirational women who paved their own way in science
through determination and hard work. Girl Power!—K. D. & S. R. J.

For Sylvie and my Einstein—V. H.

Cece Loves Science
Text copyright © 2018 by Kimberly Derting and Shelli R. Johannes
Illustrations copyright © 2018 by Vashti Harrison
All rights reserved. Printed in the United States of America. For
information address HarperCollins Children's Books, a division of
HarperCollins Publishers, 195 Broadway, New York, NY 10007.
www.harpercollinschildrens.com

The full-color art was created in Adobe Photoshop™.
The text type is Candida.

Library of Congress Cataloging-in-Publication Data is available.
ISBN 978-0-06-249961-5 (pbk.)

21 22 23 24 PC 10 9 8 7 6 5
First paperback edition, 2020.
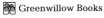 Greenwillow Books